Robotic Scorpion

By
Melissa Stewart

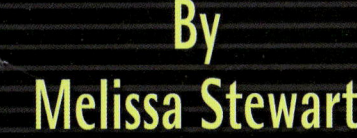

For Colin

Silver Dolphin Books
An imprint of the Advantage Publishers Group
5880 Oberlin Drive, San Diego, CA 92121-4794
www.silverdolphinbooks.com

Text copyright © becker&mayer!, 2004
Cover and interior illustrations copyright © becker&mayer!, 2004

Copyright under International, Pan American, and Universal Copyright Conventions. All rights reserved. No part of this book may be reproduced or transmitted in any form or by any means, electronic or mechanical, including photocopying, recording, or by any information storage-and-retrieval system, without written permission from the copyright holder.

Robotic Scorpion is produced by becker&mayer!,
Bellevue, Washington.
www.beckermayer.com

If you have questions or comments about this product, send an e-mail to infobm@beckermayer.com.

ISBN-13: 978-1-59223-211-6
ISBN-10: 1-59223-211-6

Produced, manufactured, and assembled in China

4 5 6 7 8 10 09 08 07 06

06322

Edited by Ben Grossblatt
Art direction and design by J. Max Steinmetz
Illustrations by Roberto Campus, Roger Harris, Erik Omtvedt, & J. Max Steinmetz
Product & toy design by Chris Tanner & Andy Young
Technical assembly illustrations by J. Max Steinmetz
Production management by Pirkko Terao & Katie Stephens
Cover photography by Keith Megay
Facts checked by Paul Beck & Melody Moss
Special thanks to Jan Ove Rein for generous scorpion assistance, and to Roger D. Quinn for his Whegs enthusiasm

Image credits

Every effort has been made to correctly attribute all the material reproduced in this book.
We will be happy to correct any errors in future editions.

Pages 6–7: Scorpion mother with babies © Patrick Bultel, courtesy of Patrick Bultel.
Pages 8–9: Da Vinci surgical robot courtesy of Intuitive Surgical; Factory robot courtesy of Monte Hight, Robochopper, Inc.
Pages 12–13: DANTE II courtesy of Carnegie Mellon University and NASA; Velcro (magnified image), © Dr. Elaine Humphrey, used with permission.
Pages 16–17: Scorpion (shown with nervous system overlay) © Jan Ove Rein, The Scorpion Files, courtesy of Jan Ove Rein; Cockroach on platform courtesy of Robert Full and the Poly-PEDAL Lab.
Pages 18–19: Comet II © Dr. Kenzo Nonami, courtesy of Dr. Kenzo Nonami, Chiba University.
Pages 20–21: RHex © 2003 Peter Menzel/menzelphoto.com, used with permission; Sprawl © Mark Cutkosky, Stanford University Biomimetic Robotics Lab, courtesy of Mark Cutkosky; Spider-bot courtesy of NASA/JPL-Caltech; Boadicea courtesy of Annika Pfluger, MIT.
Pages 22–23: RoboLobster © Jan Witting/Northeastern University, courtesy of Joseph Ayers; MFI © Ron Fearing, courtesy of Ron Fearing, University of California at Berkeley; Ariel courtesy of Julie Shinnick, iRobot Corporation.

Scorpions & Robots

Imagine a creature that can withstand extreme temperatures—from below freezing to a brutal 120°F—and survive in almost any environment on earth. Would you believe a scorpion can do that? They're found all over the planet, and they're among the best-adapted animals in the world.

Now imagine a creature that can mow your lawn, vacuum your living room, guard a museum, build a car, drive a train, defuse a bomb, or explore the surface of Mars, all without oxygen or food. That creature is a robot!

A robot is a machine that has movable parts and can be programmed to do a job by itself. Like people, robots can take in information from their surroundings and process it. But robots don't actually think the way people do. They can only react in ways that have been programmed into their computer brain.

Combine a robot with a scorpion and you've got your robotic scorpion.

TABLE OF CONTENTS

Scorpion Fact File	4
The Scoop on Scorpions	6
Relying on Robots	8
Robot Anatomy	10
Learning from Nature	12
The Wonders of Walking	14
Building Better Robots	16
The Perfect Scorpionbot	18
Six-Legged Robots	20
Swimmers, Creepers, and Fliers	22
A Robot Named Scorpion	24
Assembly Instructions	26
Robotic Scorpion Experiments	32

Scorpion Fact File

What's so great about scorpions? Everything! The way they look and the way they act are perfectly attuned to where they live. Their physical features and behaviors help them survive in the world's harshest environments, avoid detection, and fight off enemies. They're stealthy, fierce, and strong.

SCORPIONS BELONG TO A GROUP OF INVERTEBRATES CALLED ARACHNIDS. SPIDERS, MITES, AND TICKS ARE ALSO ARACHNIDS.

old-timers
Scorpions were probably one of the first animals to live on land. They've found a way to survive on earth for more than 420 million years!

eyes
Most scorpions have between two and twelve eyes, depending on the species. (Some scorpions have no eyes.) Scorpion eyes don't work like human eyes. A scorpion's eyes can detect light and movement, but they can't see colors or form images.

chelicerae (kill-ISS-uh-rye)
A scorpion's fangs, or chelicerae, are perfectly designed to tear apart prey and place the pieces in its mouth.

chelae (KEE-lye)
A scorpion uses these two strong, clawlike pincers at the ends of its front legs (which are called pedipalps) to locate and grasp prey. Some scorpions can lift more than 20 times their body weight with one chela.

Tough Customers
Over time, scorpions have developed adaptations that allow them to endure temperatures below the freezing point and above 120 degrees Fahrenheit. They can live for up to a year with no food, require very little water or oxygen, and can withstand high-energy radiation. These characteristics make them perfectly suited for life in almost all of the world's habitats.

stinger
A scorpion's stinger is a hollow tube at the end of its tail. Two sacs in the stinger store venom until it is needed. (Scorpions can also choose to sting without injecting venom into their victims.) Most scorpions deliver a sting less severe than a bee's, but about 25 species have venom strong enough to kill a person.

exoskeleton
A scorpion's body is protected by a hard, rigid exoskeleton. This outer armor is coated with a waxy substance that locks moisture into the animal's body. As a young scorpion grows, it must molt, or shed its exoskeleton, five or six times.

green glow
A scorpion's exoskeleton contains a substance that glows under ultraviolet light. Scorpion seekers carry portable "black lights" at night and look for a green glow. Even the fossilized remains of long-dead scorpions will glow in ultraviolet light.

walking legs
A scorpion has four pairs of walking legs. Tiny claws at the end of each leg help a scorpion stabilize itself and climb over rocks.

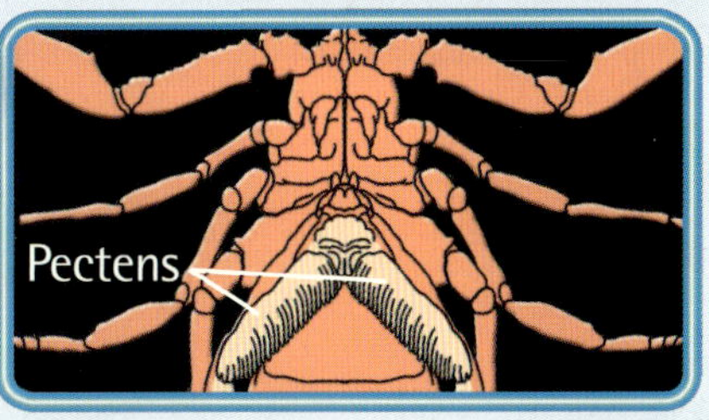

pectens
These comblike structures on a scorpion's underside are important sensory organs. They detect vibration from the ground and sense the temperature and water content of the ground. Pectens also function as a scorpion's nose, picking up incredibly faint smells.

Rule of Thumb
A generalization about scorpions and their venom goes like this: Scorpion species with thick, heavy pedipalps tend to have less poisonous venom.

Scorpion species with narrow pedipalps tend to have more poisonous venom. If a scorpion has potent venom, it doesn't need powerful claws.

The Scoop on Scorpions

About 1,200 species of scorpions live on earth today.

Where the Scorpions Are
Most species live in the tropics, but some can be found as far north as Canada and central Europe or as far south as the tips of South America and Africa.

We generally think of scorpions as desert dwellers, but they also live on salty beaches, in rain forests, and atop tall mountains. They have been found under snow-covered rocks in the Himalayas, in the crevices of Hawaiian pineapples, and in pitch-black caves more than 2,000 feet underground.

The Scorpion Lifestyle
No matter where a scorpion lives, it spends most of its time hiding in burrows or under rocks or bark. This can make it hard for scorpions to find mates, so when it's time to reproduce, females release a chemical that attracts males.

After mating, female scorpions keep their eggs inside their bodies for up to a year. Then as many as a hundred little scorpions are born at once. The newborns climb onto their mother's back, where they will be safe from predators until they are large enough to survive on their own.

Scorpions live in environments all over the world.

A scorpion walking in deep sand uses its tail and chelae for traction.

Traction Control
Because scorpions often travel over difficult terrain like deep sand, they need help to keep their footing. When climbing in sand, some scorpions will lay their tails flat on the ground to get more traction. And some walk with their chelae open. When they feel something to grab onto, a stick for instance, they'll close their chelae around it and pull themselves forward.

A scorpion dines on an insect.

what's on the menu?
When a scorpion gets hungry, it emerges from its hiding place at dusk and waits for insects, spiders, snails, or other scorpions to pass by. Once in a while, a scorpion may also set its sights on a small bird, rodent, lizard, or frog. If nothing passes by, the scorpion heads home at dawn.

Come and Get It!
Because scorpions have efficient digestive systems and are good at conserving food energy, they may only have to eat three or four times a year. As a result, many live more than five years and a few may live to the ripe old age of 25.

Tiny sensory hairs on the scorpion's pedipalps can detect the motion of flying insects, while pectens pick up vibrations on or below the ground. When a scorpion detects a potential meal, it ambushes the prey and seizes it. If the victim puts up a fight, the scorpion zaps it with its stinger. Holding the prey in its claws, the scorpion tears it apart with its chelicerae and then sucks out the juices.

Relying on Robots

Because robots can move and react to changes in their environment—and are sometimes designed to have the best traits of animals—they sometimes seem like intelligent beings. If a robot detects a problem, it can avoid (or even solve) it.

For example, you don't need to push or steer a robotic lawnmower because it powers itself and senses when it has reached the edge of your lawn. And workers can leave a museum at the end of the day, knowing a robotic security guard will call for help if it detects a fire or a burglar.

Oldies but Goodies

The idea of man-made helpers has been around for centuries. The ancient Greek poet Homer described mechanical maidens made of gold. The robotic ladies attended to their masters' every need. According to medieval Jewish legend, a magical chant could bring to life clay servants called golems. In 1495, the Italian artist and scientist Leonardo da Vinci drew plans for a mechanical man (shown to the right) in his notebooks.

dr. Robot

Robots have even moved into the operating room. These remote-control surgeons help patients (and doctors) by performing the many delicate movements that an operation requires. The human surgeon uses high-tech controls to direct the robot. Special tips on the robo-doctor's arms even let it tie stitches!

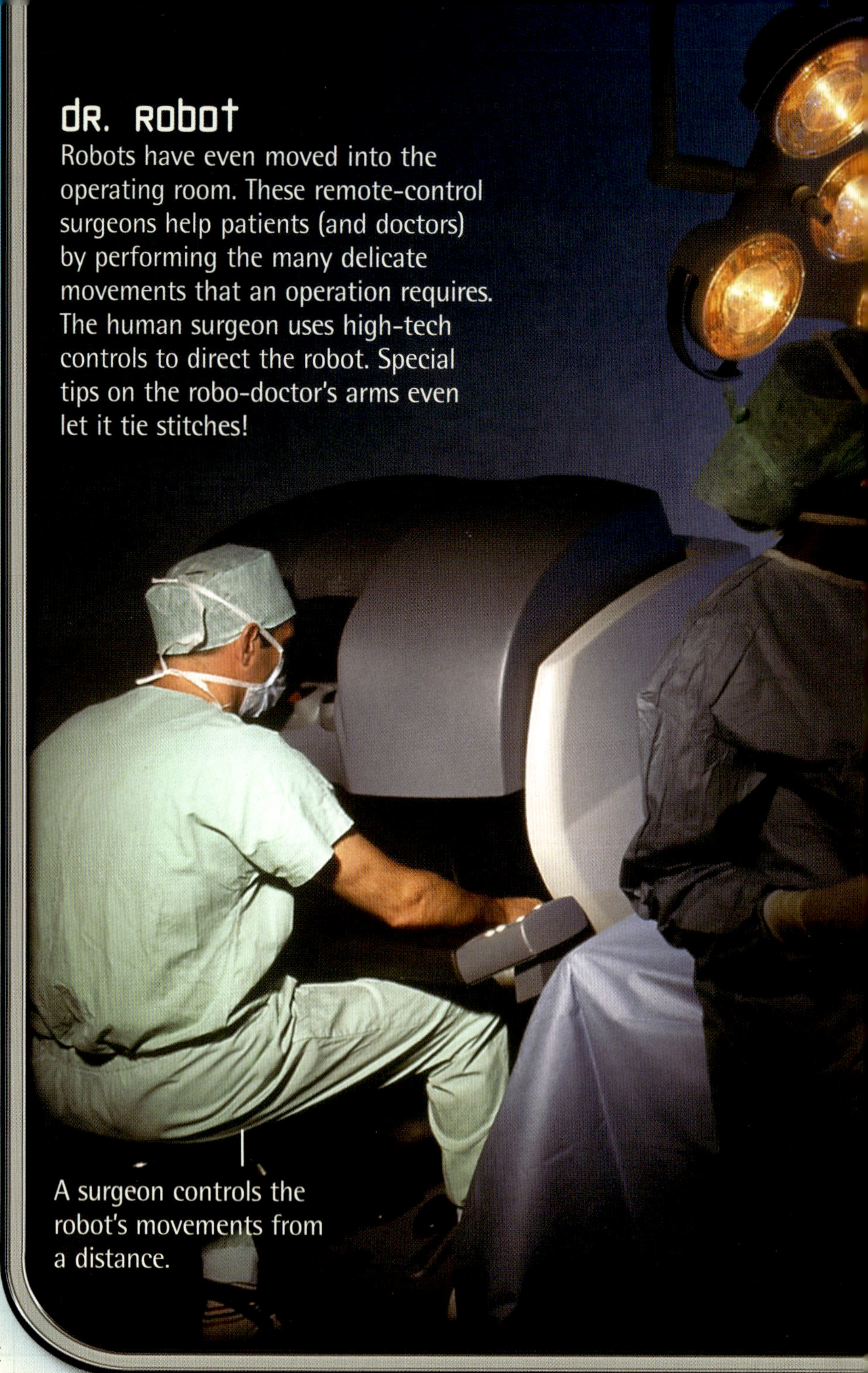

A surgeon controls the robot's movements from a distance.

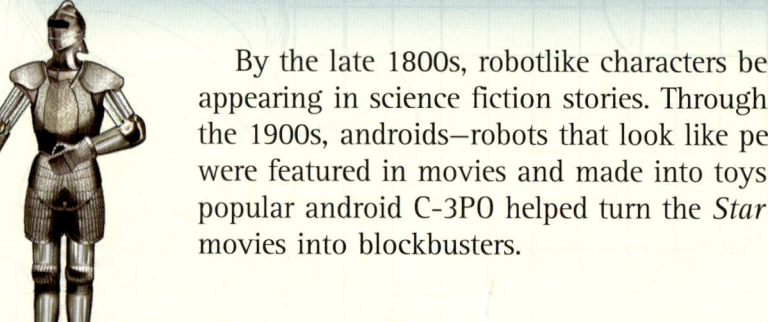

By the late 1800s, robotlike characters began appearing in science fiction stories. Throughout the 1900s, androids—robots that look like people—were featured in movies and made into toys. The popular android C-3PO helped turn the *Star Wars* movies into blockbusters.

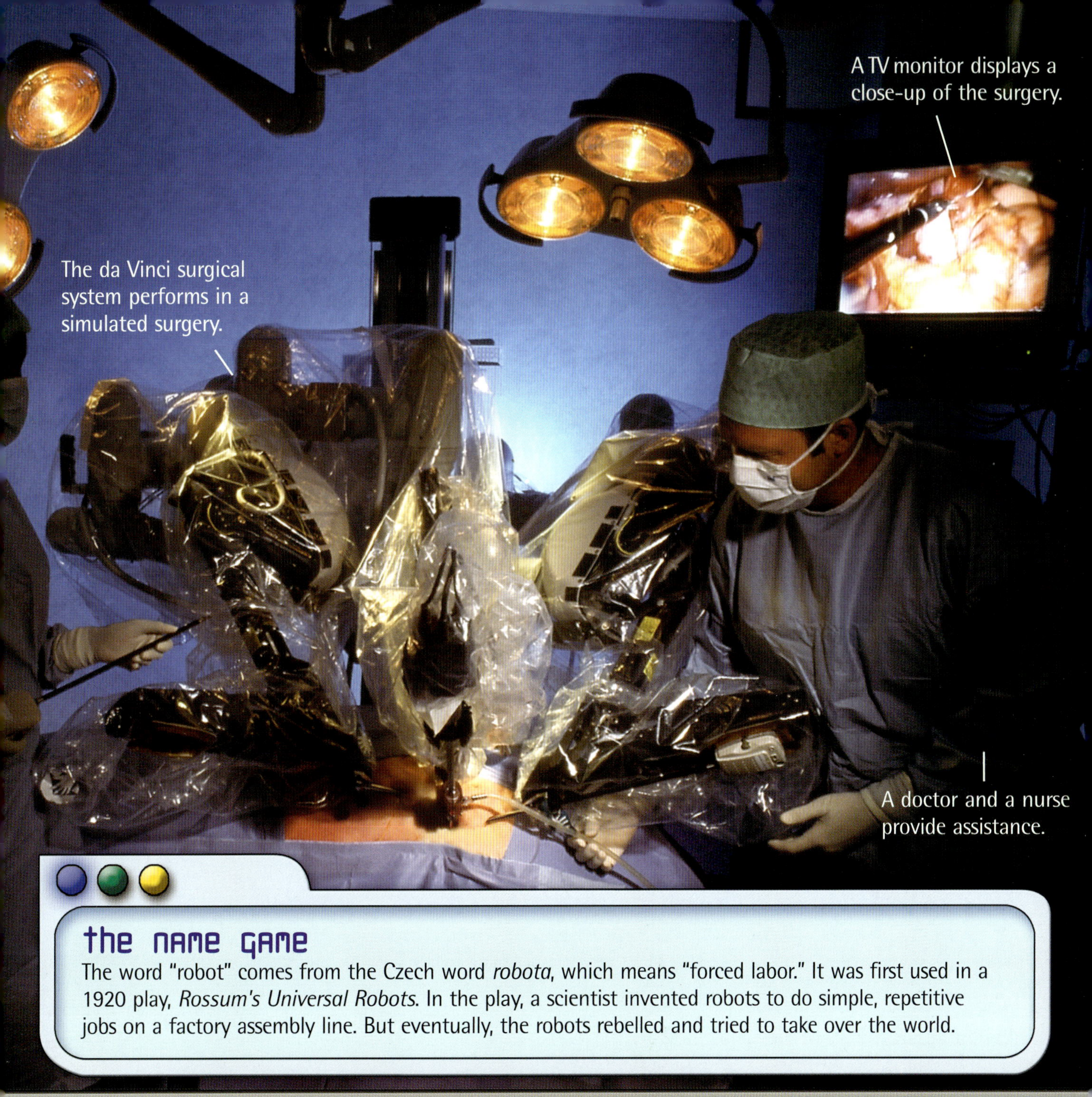

The da Vinci surgical system performs in a simulated surgery.

A TV monitor displays a close-up of the surgery.

A doctor and a nurse provide assistance.

the name game
The word "robot" comes from the Czech word *robota*, which means "forced labor." It was first used in a 1920 play, *Rossum's Universal Robots*. In the play, a scientist invented robots to do simple, repetitive jobs on a factory assembly line. But eventually, the robots rebelled and tried to take over the world.

Best Workers in the World

Most robots do jobs that people can't do—or don't want to. Name a boring or dangerous job. Somewhere, a robot is probably doing it. Robots have no trouble working in blistering heat, freezing cold, or places that smell bad. They can explore active volcanoes, spend days tracking enemy soldiers in the desert, and clean up toxic chemical spills.

Robots are good workers because they don't take vacations or stop to eat lunch. All they need to do their job is a power source and regular maintenance. And robots don't mind doing the same boring or messy job day after day, week after week, year after year. In factories, they arrange chocolates in boxes, spray-paint cars, and attach tiny wires to computer chips. More than 700,000 talented robots work in the world's factories!

Robot Anatomy

Some robots can scurry across the desert like scorpions, while others whiz through the sky like flies. Despite these differences, all robots have three important features: a controller, sensors, and actuators.

Controller
A robot's controller is like an animal's brain. It usually contains a computer that can run software programs by itself. These programs have all the instructions the robot needs to do its job.

Sensors
A robot's sensors are like eyes, ears, nose, and skin. They collect information about the robot's surroundings and send electric messages to the controller. These messages help the robot figure out where its parts are, where it's going, and what's happening around it.

Actuators
A robot's actuators are its muscles. They control the robot's legs, arms, hands, wheels, and other movable parts.

the five senses and beyond
Some robots have video cameras for seeing. Some have microphones for hearing. And others have sensors for measuring temperature or pressure. Even though most robotic sensors mimic the senses we're familiar with, some detect things our bodies can't, such as magnetic fields or ultrasonic sound waves.

A firefighting robot uses tracks and special sensors to do its job.

ROBOTICS ENGINEERS USE THE TERM "DEGREE OF FREEDOM" (DOF) TO DESCRIBE HOW ROBOT PARTS MOVE. EACH DOF IS ONE TYPE OF MOTION. YOUR WRIST HAS THREE DOFS: IT CAN MOVE UP AND DOWN, SIDE TO SIDE, AND AROUND IN A CIRCLE.

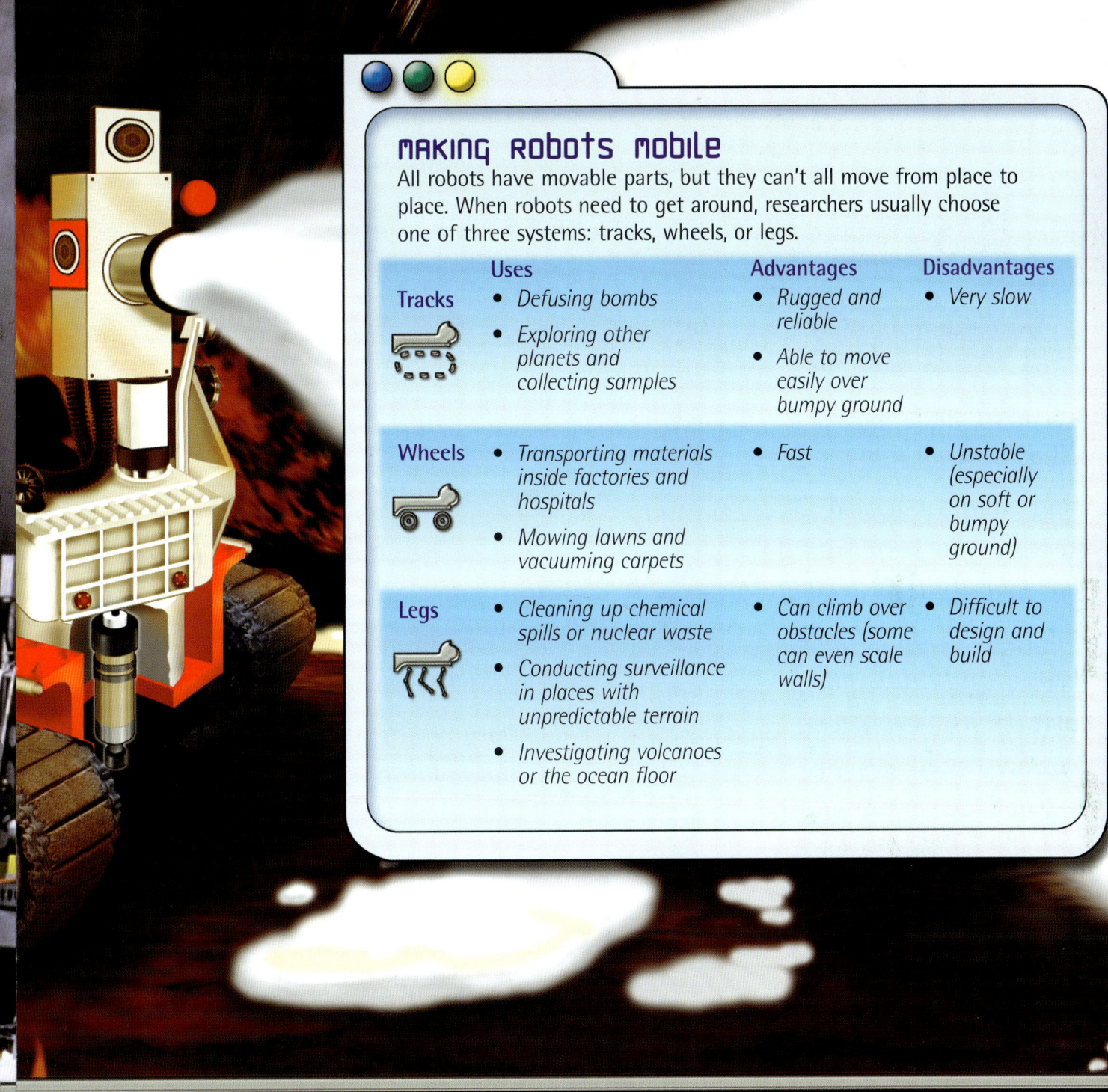

Making Robots Mobile

All robots have movable parts, but they can't all move from place to place. When robots need to get around, researchers usually choose one of three systems: tracks, wheels, or legs.

	Uses	Advantages	Disadvantages
Tracks	• Defusing bombs • Exploring other planets and collecting samples	• Rugged and reliable • Able to move easily over bumpy ground	• Very slow
Wheels	• Transporting materials inside factories and hospitals • Mowing lawns and vacuuming carpets	• Fast	• Unstable (especially on soft or bumpy ground)
Legs	• Cleaning up chemical spills or nuclear waste • Conducting surveillance in places with unpredictable terrain • Investigating volcanoes or the ocean floor	• Can climb over obstacles (some can even scale walls)	• Difficult to design and build

Robots on the Move

Many actuators are powered by electricity, just like TVs, refrigerators, and light bulbs. But some robotic parts get their energy from systems that compress air or liquids.

Compressed air is especially good for powering robot legs and other parts that need to respond quickly. It is also used in jackhammers and drills. Using compressed air in this way is called pneumatics (noo-MAD-iks). Compressed liquids are the best power source for robot parts that lift heavy objects. They are also used to mold large sheets of metal for airplane exteriors and to lift materials at construction sites. Using compressed liquids like this is called hydraulics (hi-DRAW-liks). Scorpions use hydraulics, too: A scorpion's muscles can only curl the legs inward. To straighten its legs, a scorpion has to pump blood into them.

The Wonders of Walking

Walking requires the ability to coordinate complex movements. And depending on the walker, it can also demand very good balance. The designers of walking robots face many challenges in creating machines that walk steadily and quickly.

WALKING MAY SEEM EASY TO YOU NOW, BUT IT WASN'T SO SIMPLE WHEN YOU WERE A BABY. NEWBORNS ARE HELPLESS. THEY HAVE TO LEARN HOW TO TURN OVER, HOW TO CRAWL, HOW TO STAND UP, AND FINALLY, HOW TO WALK.

Harder than It Looks

During their first 12 to 18 months, babies learn many important lessons about balance and coordination. The engineers who design robots with legs experience the same kinds of challenges. They have to figure out how to keep their mechanical devices balanced and oriented, even on rugged terrain.

By studying biomechanics (by-oh-mih-CAN-iks)—the way forces act on our muscles and bones when we move and the way our bodies respond to those forces—engineers have discovered that walking on two legs takes a lot of brainpower.

Building a controller and system of sensors complex enough to keep a two-legged robot balanced is very difficult and expensive. That's why so many engineers are now building robots with more than two legs.

Six legs can keep a robot stable during all phases of walking. Even in the middle of a step, with three feet off the ground, the robot is still supported by a sturdy tripod of legs.

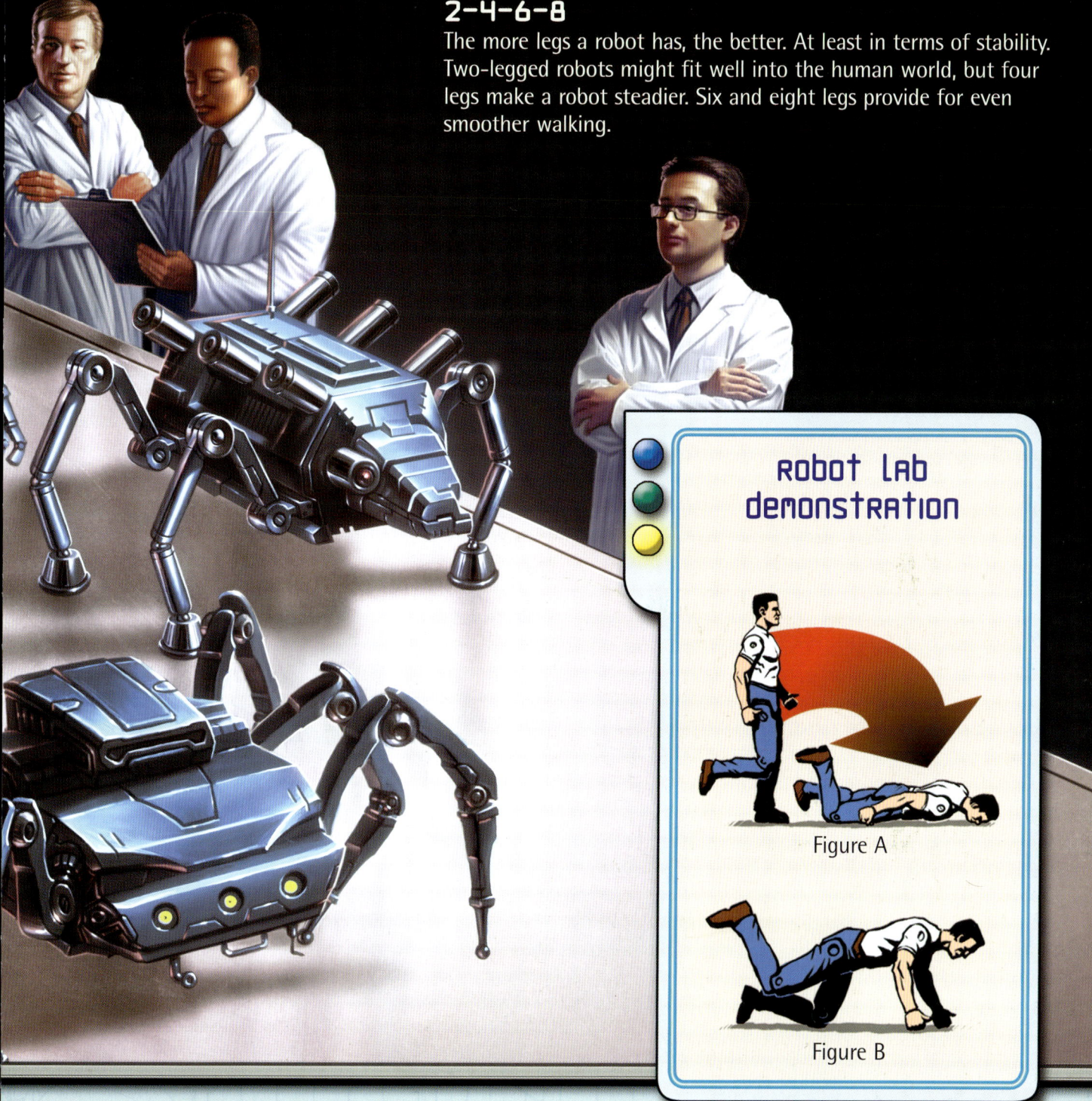

2-4-6-8

The more legs a robot has, the better. At least in terms of stability. Two-legged robots might fit well into the human world, but four legs make a robot steadier. Six and eight legs provide for even smoother walking.

robot Lab demonstration

Figure A

Figure B

Your Own Robot Lab

Find a two-legged action figure with movable arms and legs. Stand it upright on an uncarpeted floor or other smooth surface. Move one of its legs up, as if it were about to take a step (see Figure A above). What happens when you let go of the action figure?

Now bend the action figure over, so both hands and both feet are touching the floor. Lift one leg up (see Figure B). What happens when you let go?

When the action figure is standing and you lift one leg, the toy has only one contact point with the floor, so it's very unstable. But when it is positioned on all fours and you lift one leg, the toy still has three contact points with the floor.

Like the action figure, a robot with four legs is steadier than a robot with just two legs. And a robot with six or eight legs is even more stable.

Building Better Robots

When it comes to building better robots, invertebrates (in-VERD-uh-brits)—animals without backbones—are the biomimetic models of choice. Scorpions, spiders, insects, lobsters, and crabs are simple animals that have adapted to survive in environments all over the world. Even though their nervous systems are less complex than the average home computer, they can do most of the things engineers would like robots to do.

The Brains of the Operation

Scorpion brains are very small. Some can be less than one millimeter across. That's about one twenty-fifth of an inch. But scorpions are just as intelligent as they need to be, and they display great agility and hunting skills. And for such "simple" animals, their nervous systems are complex and elegant.

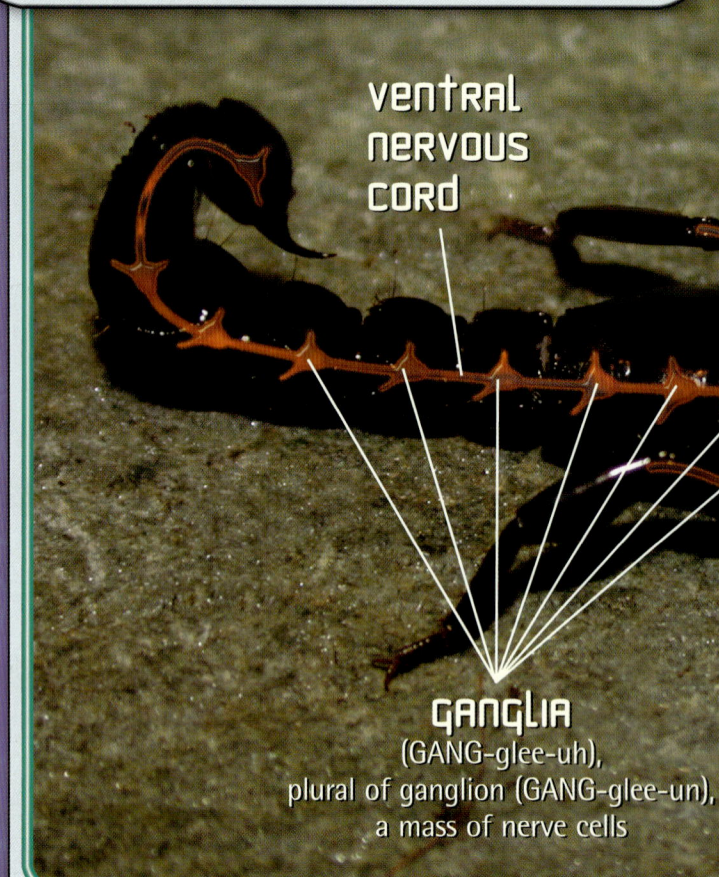

ventral nervous cord

ganglia (GANG-glee-uh), plural of ganglion (GANG-glee-un), a mass of nerve cells

Out of Balance

To find out how invertebrates do all the things they do, scientists have spent many hours patiently studying the animals themselves. In one series of experiments, they built a platform with computerized sensors. When a crab, cockroach, or centipede ran across the platform, the sensors measured the creature's speed, leg and body movements, and how those movements related to forces acting on the animal's body. These experiments also used a high-speed video camera to film the animals running. Scientists analyzed the images by looking at one frame at a time.

The results of the experiments surprised many scientists. It turns out that animals do not remain perfectly balanced during all phases of walking or running. As an animal walks or runs, its body swings like a pendulum and bounces like a pogo stick. This method of moving is the secret behind an animal's

16

who needs a backbone?

Invertebrates are masters at interpreting and reacting to their surroundings. They can communicate with one another, and they can act alone or as part of a group. But most importantly, they can move across rugged terrain quickly and easily—dashing forward, scurrying backward, scooting sideways, and scrambling over rocks.

brain

insect data

A cockroach running on a special platform in the University of California at Berkeley's Poly-PEDAL Lab can give scientists information about biomechanics.

speed and flexibility. It allows an animal to stay balanced, on average, over a step or a couple of steps, but not at every moment.

If an animal's body doesn't need to be balanced at every moment, it can leap up to cover more ground in less time. It can also squeeze through narrow openings, stretch out a leg to reach a distant foothold, and jump over obstacles.

For many years, this secret of nature gave animals a leg up on robots—but not anymore. Using the conclusions from research on invertebrate biomechanics, engineers are now developing robotic actuators that are both sturdy and flexible, so they can react like living muscle tissue.

WHEN A CENTIPEDE RUNS, IT CAN TEMPORARILY TEETER ON JUST THREE OF ITS FORTY-FOUR LEGS!

The Perfect Scorpionbot

If you wanted to make a robot that worked just like a scorpion, it would need some ingenious features. Here's a sampling of the gear any high-quality, true-to-life robot scorpion would need.

Motion-Detecting Vision

Real scorpions don't have very good vision. Most scorpions are nocturnal (they're up and about at nighttime), so you might think they'd need excellent sight to get around. You might expect that they'd have eyes as sensitive to light as cat or owl eyes. But they don't. Their eyes are useful for detecting motion and light, but not for seeing the way we do.

Robot designers have already created visual sensors for robots that work this way. Some are designed to mimic the motion-detecting abilities of fly eyes. A robotic helicopter in the works uses the principles of insect vision as a model for the way it sees the world.

Joints
Hydraulic joints for moving heavy legs

Gripping Power

A scorpion's clawlike chelae function as its hands. They grasp prey, pull the scorpions up sandy slopes, and even play an important role in the scorpion "mating dance."

Robots with arms can use a wide variety of "hands," called end effectors. End effectors are tools to let robots perform many different tasks, such as welding, drilling, painting, grinding, and gripping. Grippers are common end effectors. Some look like an alien's delicate three-fingered hand, and some resemble a scorpion's chela. And like a scorpion's chela, these grippers can be powerful. Some are capable of 600 pounds of gripping force. (That's more than 100 times stronger than a human grip.)

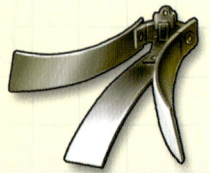   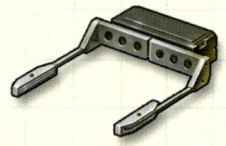 

A sampling of robotic end effectors

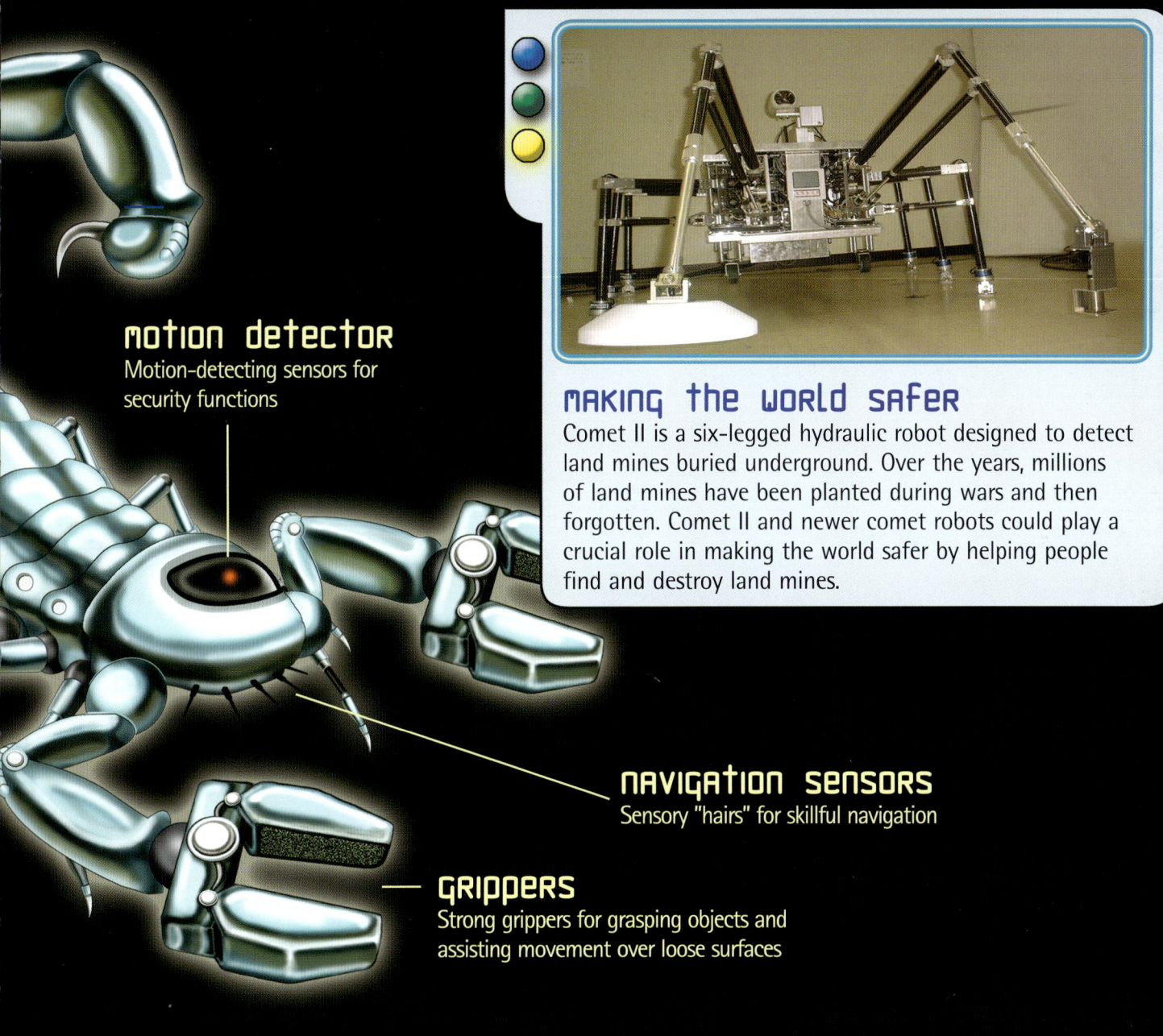

motion detector
Motion-detecting sensors for security functions

making the world safer
Comet II is a six-legged hydraulic robot designed to detect land mines buried underground. Over the years, millions of land mines have been planted during wars and then forgotten. Comet II and newer comet robots could play a crucial role in making the world safer by helping people find and destroy land mines.

navigation sensors
Sensory "hairs" for skillful navigation

grippers
Strong grippers for grasping objects and assisting movement over loose surfaces

Real Feel
Scorpions don't need good vision because they have other ways of sensing their environment. That's where pectens and sensory hairs on legs and pedipalps (called trichobothria) come in. Using these touch sensors, scorpions can get around in almost any terrain.

Thanks to researchers, robots can now get around in the same way. Cockroaches are a favorite model for robot-makers. Cockroaches have antennae for feeling their way along and, like scorpions, they have sensory hairs that work like motion detectors. Sprawlette is one roachbot with an antenna-like feeler.

Fluid Movement
Like other arachnids, scorpions use a hydraulic system to straighten their legs. By pumping blood into their legs, they're able to compensate for not having the muscles needed for leg straightening.

Robots use hydraulics, too. (For smaller robots, pneumatics—power from the force of air—is more effective. The robots that use compressed liquids tend to be larger and more powerful.)

19

Six-Legged Robots

A parade of six-legged robots with names like Sprawl, RHex, and Spider-bot are all biomimetic. They walk and react like crabs, spiders, cockroaches, and centipedes.

Insect Inspiration

A series of six-legged robots built by a mechanical engineer at Case Western Reserve University in Cleveland, Ohio, was also modeled after the lowly cockroach. The most recent models in the series have small, mobile front legs perfectly suited for exploring the environment, while the large, powerful back legs were designed to propel the robot forward.

Based on these initial successes, robot engineers all over the world have begun borrowing more tricks from invertebrates. They are developing new robotic sensors that gather information about their environment in the same way as invertebrate eyes, antennae, and other sense organs. And they are creating a new generation of robotic controllers that process data just like an invertebrate's brain and nerves.

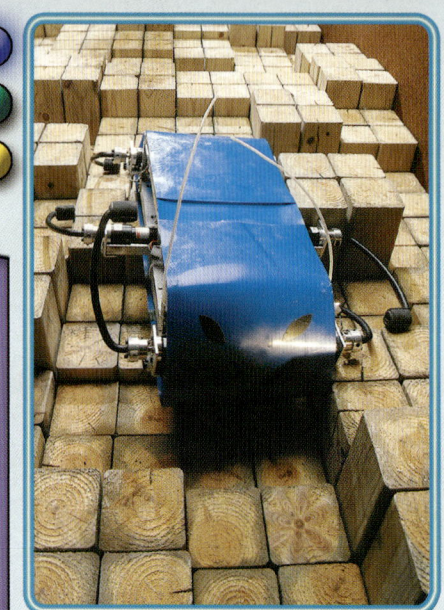

RHex
This 14-pound robot, the size of a toaster oven, was designed and built by engineers from the University of Michigan and McGill University in Montreal, Canada. Its springy legs are mounted on hip joints that rotate in a full circle, allowing the robot to walk, run, and leap over obstacles on a variety of terrains. It can even climb stairs.

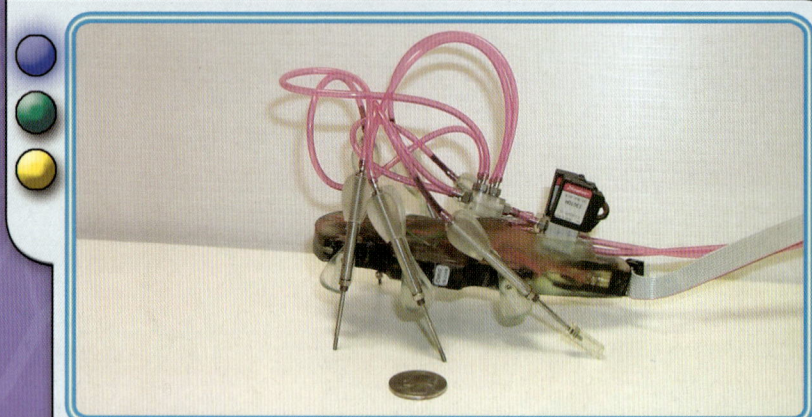

Sprawls
This family of hand-sized robots, which includes SprawlEx, Sprawlita, Mini-Sprawl, Pseudo-Sprawl, and others, was designed and built at Stanford University in Palo Alto, California. The fast, rugged robots have been used to study leg design and arrangement.

Six-Legged Whegs

While robots with six or more legs tend to be more stable and maneuverable than robots with two or four, there might be something even better. Researchers at Case Western have developed robots that walk with what they call "Whegs," or wheel-legs.

A Wheg robot, such as Case Western's Whegs-I or Whegs-II, walk-rolls on six legs, each resembling a bicycle wheel without the rim. These robots are

spider-bot
Even though Spider-bot has six legs instead of eight, it looks very similar to a real spider. Designed by researchers at NASA's Jet Propulsion Laboratory in Pasadena, California, this miniature, high-tech creature may one day map the terrain on other planets or explore comets, asteroids, or the Moon. It may also help with maintenance and repairs on the International Space Station.

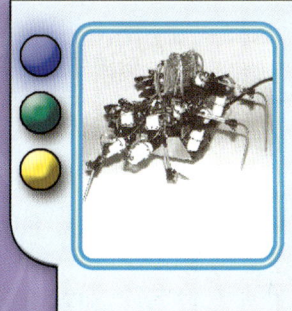

boadicea
One robot that made use of pneumatics was developed in the Mobile Robot Lab at the Massachusetts Institute of Technology (MIT).

Because Boadicea's actuators were powered by compressed air, the robot was strong and lightweight. This allowed it to walk faster and carry more weight than any other small, mobile robot built before.

faster than legged robots and can move over rougher terrain than wheeled robots can.

They walk with the typical "tripod" gait—three feet on the ground at one time—until they encounter an obstacle. Then the feet move in sync to give extra power to the robot so it can climb over the hurdle. (RHex, which resembles a Wheg in some ways, can't do this.) This is similar to the way a cockroach scrambles over obstacles in its way. The researchers have also designed Mini-Whegs-I and Jumping Mini-Whegs-I.

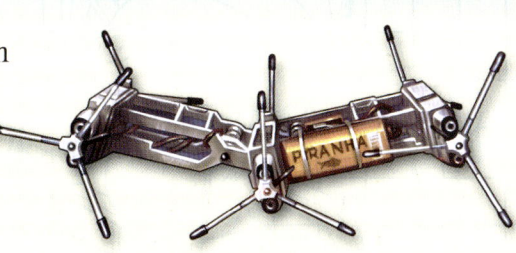

Whegs-II

Swimmers, Creepers, and Fliers

Walking insects aren't the only models robot designers use in their work. Another group of robots takes its inspiration from creatures that move in other ways. These machines swim like tuna, creep like lobsters, and fly like— you guessed it—flies.

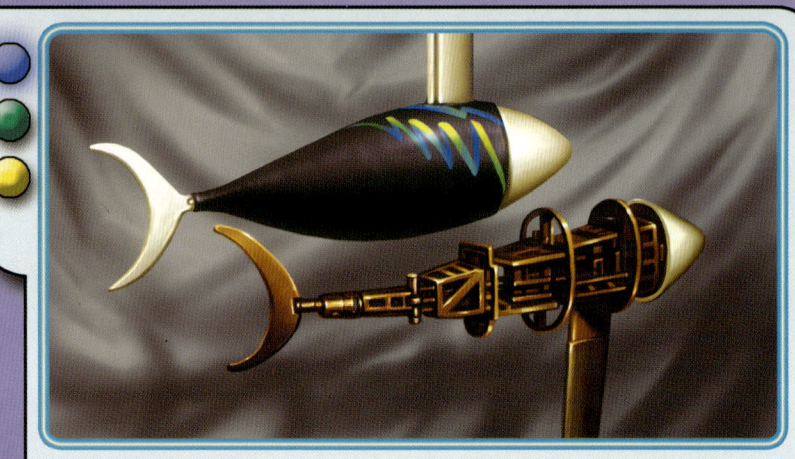

RoboTuna
Fish might look simple, but building a realistic mechanical version of one is very complex. Some fish can accelerate as fast as rockets, but scientists don't understand how they do it yet, or how they can turn as quickly as they do. Another researcher in the MIT lab is working on a RoboPike to investigate these topics further.

Mechanical Lobster
When RoboLobster is ready for action, it will be able to scamper along the ocean floor in search of sunken ships and unexploded mines.

RoboTuna
In 1993, researchers at MIT began work on RoboTuna. Their creation looks like a Lycra-skinned miniature submarine with a tail, but it slices through the water like a fish. Researchers are using the robot to study the physics of swimming. Perhaps one day it will explore coral reefs and deep ocean regions all over the world.

Mechanical Lobster
For the last twenty years, biologists at the Marine Science Center at Northeastern University in Boston have studied the shelled invertebrates in their natural habitat. They've spent many hours filming lobsters and analyzing their movements. Now they're using the data to help design RoboLobster, an eight-legged, mechanical device based on a real lobster's biomechanics and nervous system.

robofly

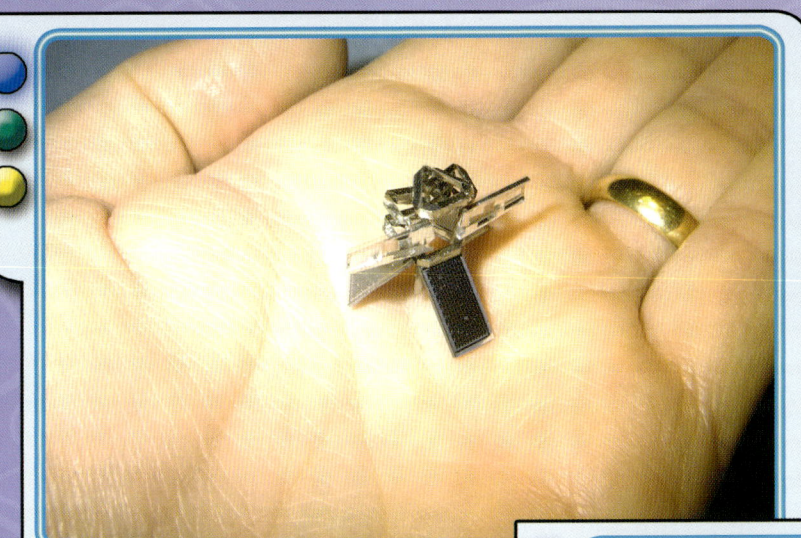

MFI is funded by the Office of Naval Research. One day, it may be used to spy on terrorists and criminals. But it could also search for survivors in earthquake rubble or burning buildings.

MFI's body is made of paper-thin stainless steel, and its Mylar wings look and feel like plastic wrap. The tiny machine weighs a little more than a housefly and is powered by lithium batteries charged by solar cells.

robotic crab

Ariel has a trick up its sleeve: if a wave knocks it over on its back, it can move upside down just as easily.

RoboFly

Meanwhile, an engineer at the University of California at Berkeley is working on MFI (Micromechanical Flying Insect).

Flies can take off and land in any direction, even upside down. They can change course in just three-thousandths of a second. And they process information at speeds that make a supercomputer seem slow. These traits make them the perfect biomimetic model for a flying robot.

Robotic Crab

Ariel is a robot designed to move like a crab and find mines underwater. Like a crab, Ariel has to be able to walk underwater and on land, over sand, pebbles, and silt. Not only that, but it has to be able to keep going in currents and crashing waves. To do that, it needs to react to changing conditions and adjust its position and the way it walks. Robot engineers call this "gait control."

A Robot Named Scorpion

SCORPIONS IN SPACE?
Officials at NASA were so impressed by Scorpion's performance that they are now testing it on Mars-like terrain. Who knows? Maybe someday soon, a Scorpion robot will blast into space.

"SCORPION" ROBOT STATS
Size: 23.6 in. x 8.7 in. x 5.9 to 13.8 in. (when standing)
Weight: 20.9 lb. (including battery)
Max. Speed: 7.9 inches per second (0.45 mph)

This brings us back to scorpions. Starting in 1999, researchers in Germany have been working on a robot called Scorpion. Like other biomimetic robots, Scorpion is modeled after its real-life namesake. In the summer of 2002, the German robot finally had a chance to strut its stuff. During a series of tests at the Southwest Research Institute in San Antonio, Texas, Scorpion proved it could handle almost any terrain or temperature.

The robot doesn't look much like a scorpion, but it walks, senses, and guides itself through its environment in similar ways.

Before Scorpion was designed, its creators carefully reviewed scorpion studies done by biologists in the 1970s. Then they spent many hours observing how real scorpions move.

Using what they learned, the researchers designed an eight-legged robot. Each leg has three actuators, giving it a wide range of motion. Both the actuators and the controller are powered by a lithium battery charged by solar cells. A network of leg sensors helps the robot detect and avoid large obstacles, determine its exact position, and navigate easily over uneven terrain.

stable stance

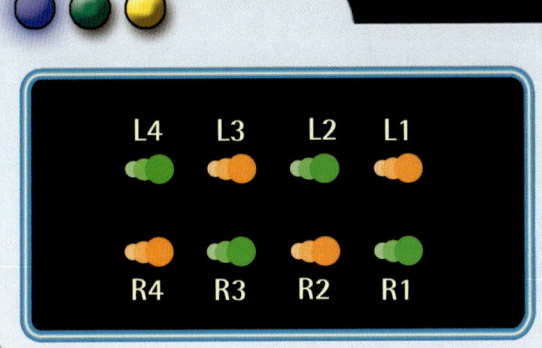

Scorpion is a very stable robot. It always balances itself on four legs. In this diagram, the left legs are labeled L1, L2, L3, and L4. The right legs are similarly labeled R1 through R4. Scorpion moves all the legs shown in orange at the same time and then all the legs shown in green. That's how it keeps four feet on the ground.

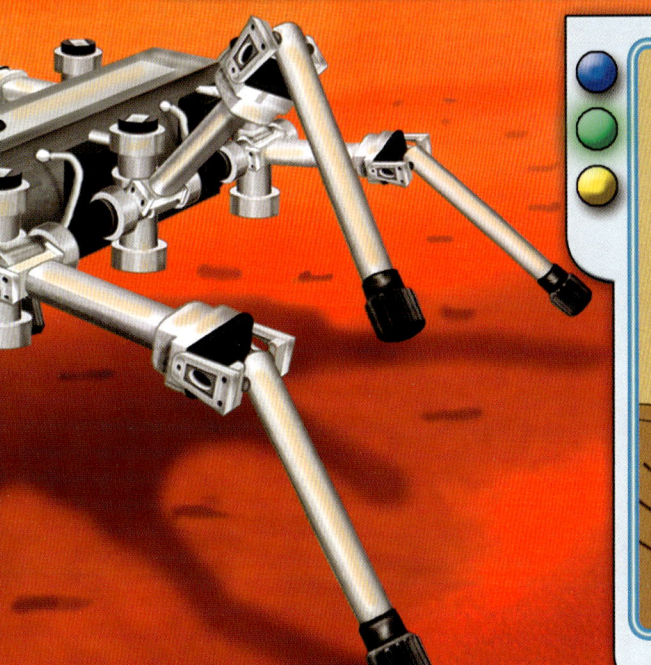

good vibrations

Researchers working for the Intelligent Robotics Research Center at Monash University in Melbourne, Australia, are testing a six-legged robot with a navigational system modeled after the scorpion's hunting technique. Touch sensors on a scorpion's legs help it detect vibrations made by insects several inches underground and pinpoint their exact location. Researchers hope that one day the robot can be used to locate victims after a natural disaster.

keep in touch

Scientists have studied sand scorpions to learn more about their ability to hunt by touch instead of sight. Scorpions can feel the vibrations caused by prey moving in sand. When these vibrations reach a hunting scorpion, they're detected by hairs on its legs. The scorpion quickly and gracefully turns in the right direction, pounces, and stings.

While Scorpion's leg design is important, the robot's most revolutionary feature is its system for guiding movements. Most of the time, Scorpion moves along with minimal sensory feedback. Since it doesn't have to process much information, very little energy is required. But as soon as the robot's sensors detect something unusual, such as an obstacle, the robot's reflexes are activated to deal with the problem.

It is this unique way of moving across rugged terrain that will eventually allow the little robot to survive for days—or even weeks—on its own. Maybe one day, the robotic scorpion will be as tough and capable as its real-life counterparts.

Now it's time for you to build your own walking robotic scorpion. Turn the page and get started!

Assembly Instructions

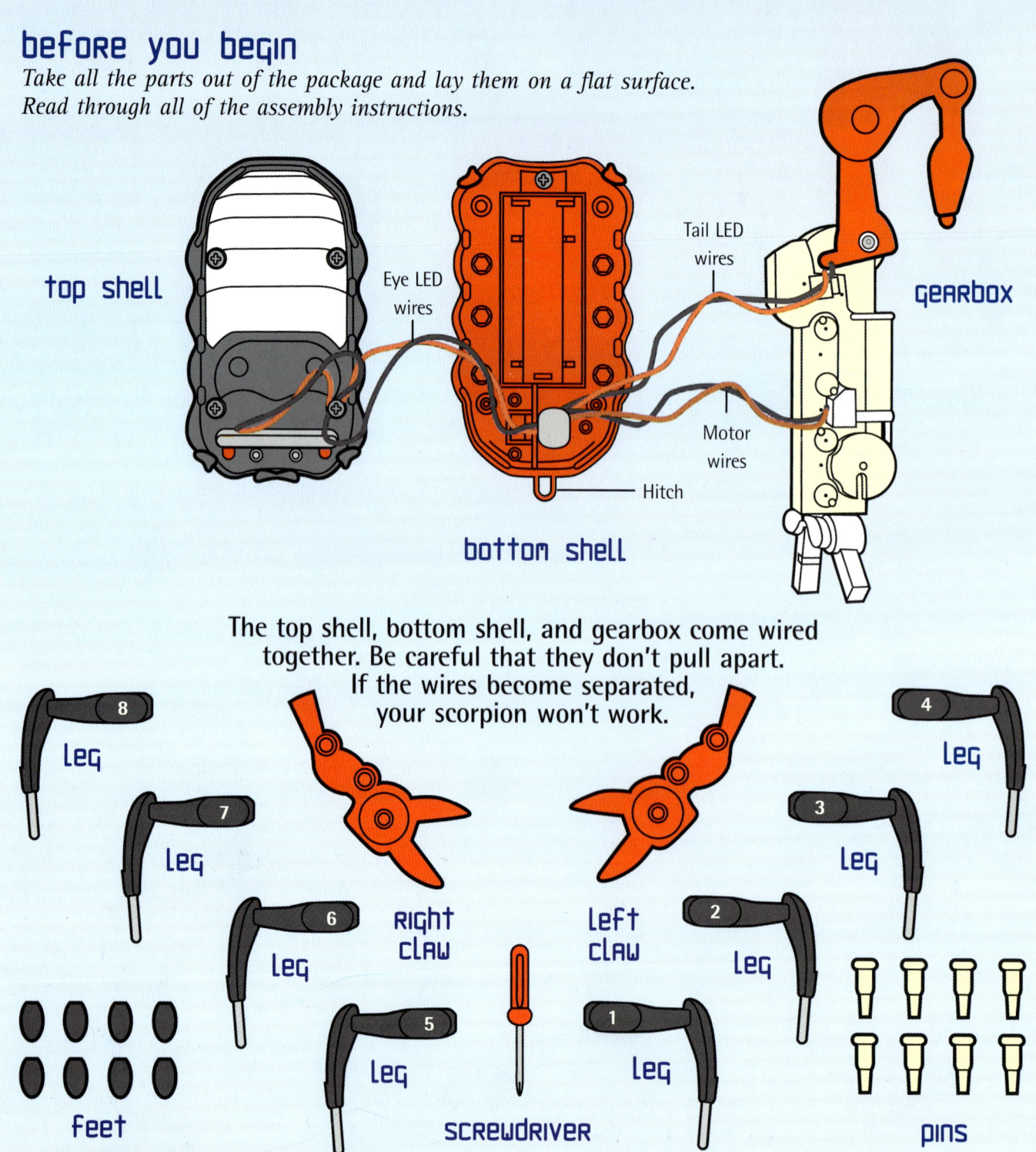

before you begin
Take all the parts out of the package and lay them on a flat surface. Read through all of the assembly instructions.

For clarity, wires aren't shown in steps 1–6.

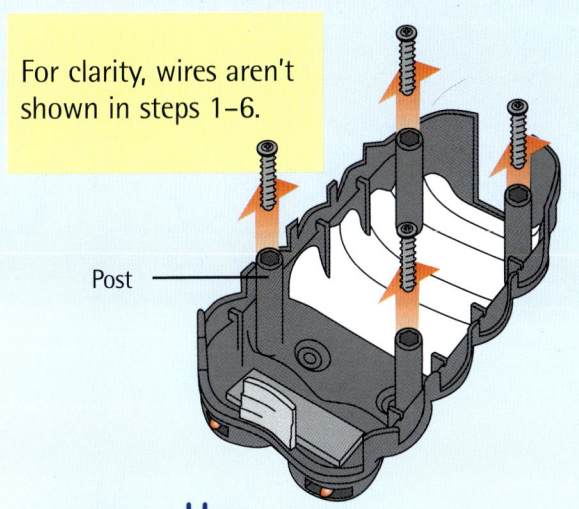

Post

1. Prep the top shell
▸ Unscrew the four screws from the posts in the inside of the top shell. Set the screws aside.

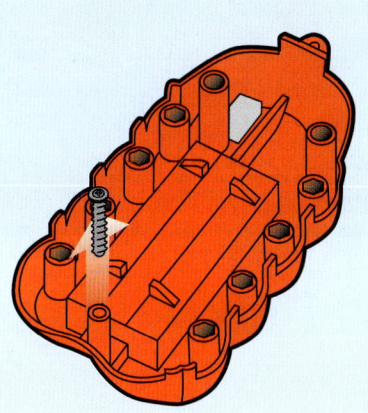

2. Prep the bottom shell
▸ Remove the screw from the inside of the bottom shell. Set the screw aside.

TIP: *Fit the hole at the front of the gearbox over the post in the bottom shell.*

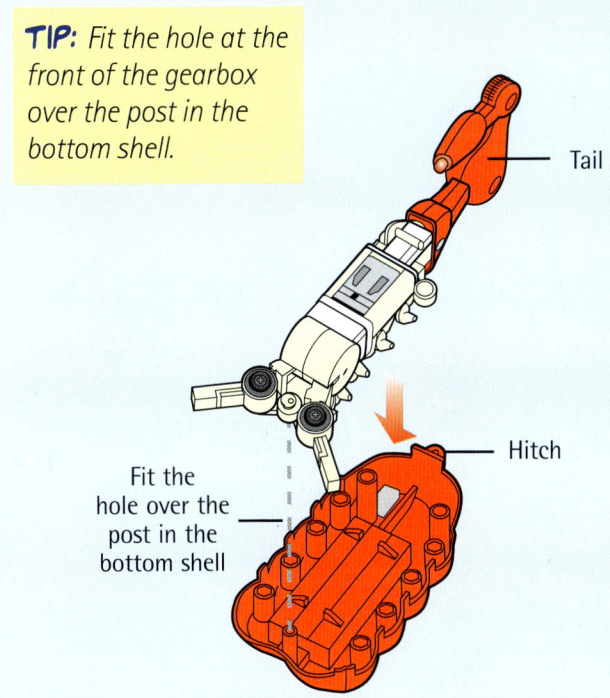

Tail

Hitch

Fit the hole over the post in the bottom shell

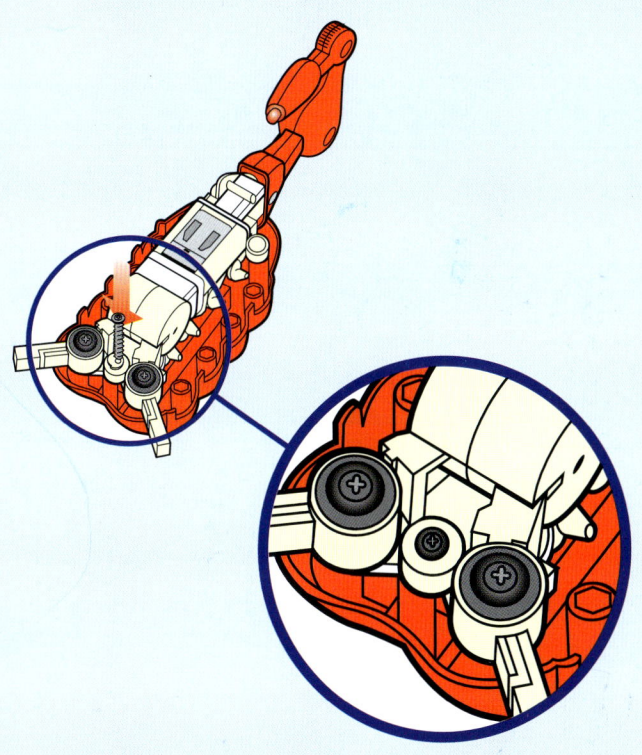

3. Install the gearbox
▸ Place the gearbox into the bottom shell. Make sure the tail end of the gearbox is pointing toward the rear of the bottom shell. (The rear of the bottom shell has a U-shaped hitch on it.)

▸ Press the gearbox into the bottom shell until it's firmly seated. Take the screw you removed in step 2 and screw it back in. This will secure the gearbox in the bottom shell.

27

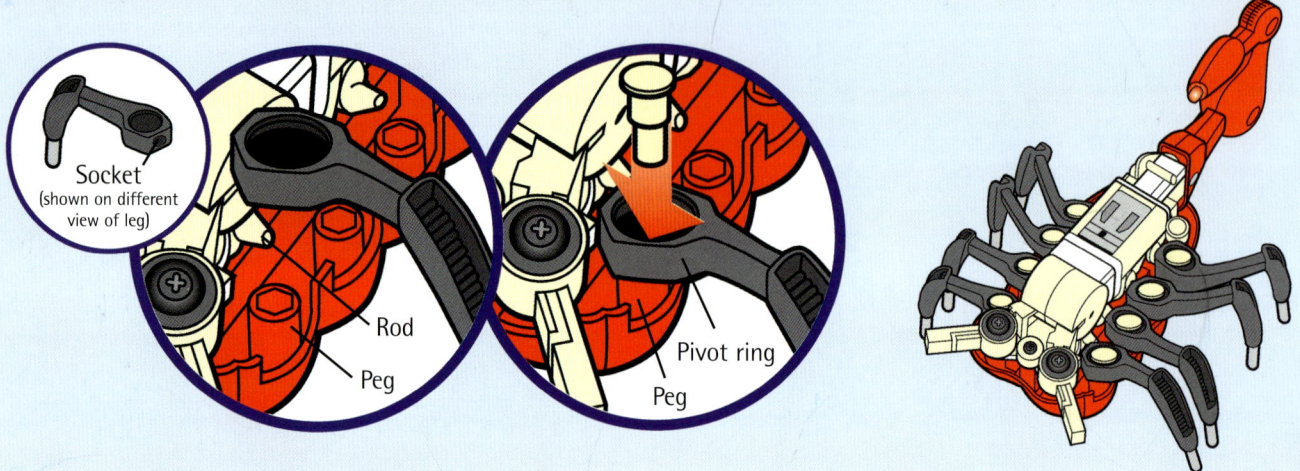

4. Attach the legs

▸ Before you can attach the legs, you'll need to make sure the pegs are clear: tuck the motor wires down between the pegs and the gearbox.

▸ Each of the legs is numbered. The gearbox rods are numbered, too. Match up the numbers on the legs with the numbers on the gearbox rods to see where to attach each leg.

▸ To attach a leg, fit the socket over the gearbox rod. Then fit the pivot ring over the peg in the bottom shell.

▸ After you've attached a leg, secure it by pressing a pin into the pivot ring.

▸ Repeat these steps for all eight legs.

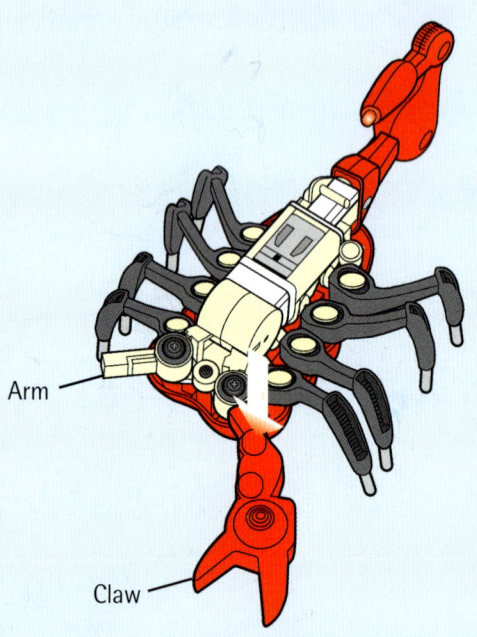
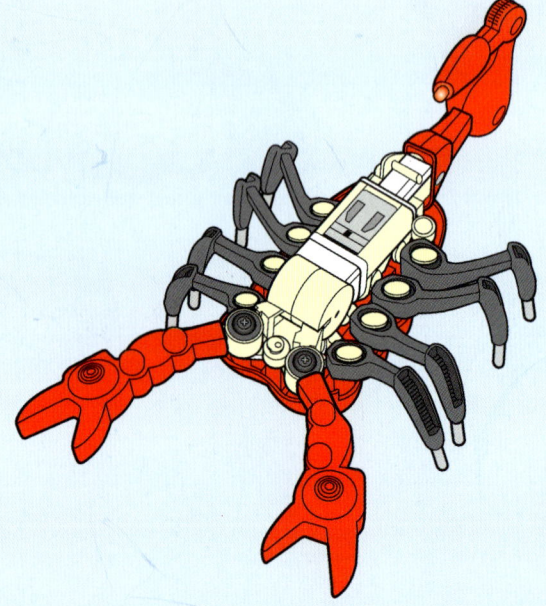

5. Attach the claws

▸ Press the left claw onto the left arm until it's fully seated. (The insides of the claws are marked L and R—for left and right.)

▸ Repeat the process with the right claw.

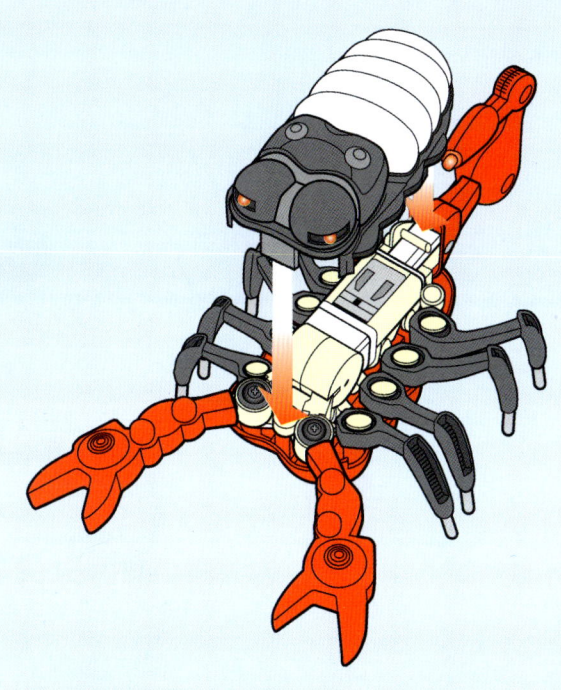

TIP: *The wires can get pinched, especially around the right rear post. Make sure the wires are clear of the hole this post fits into.*

6. Install the top shell

▸ Place the top shell onto the bottom shell. The posts on the inside of the top shell fit into the holes in the bottom shell.

▸ Make sure you don't pinch any wires between the top and bottom shells. Carefully tuck the wires inside as you place the top shell.

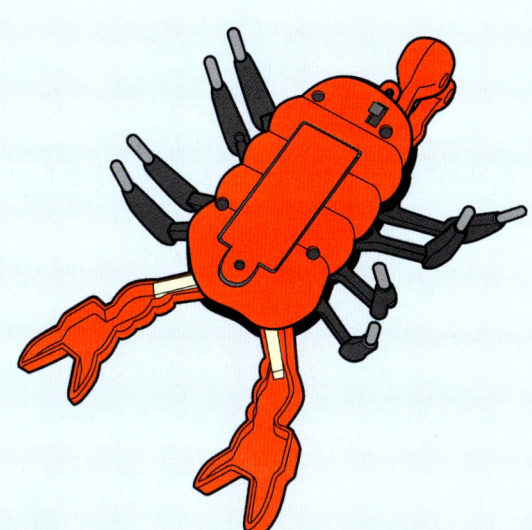
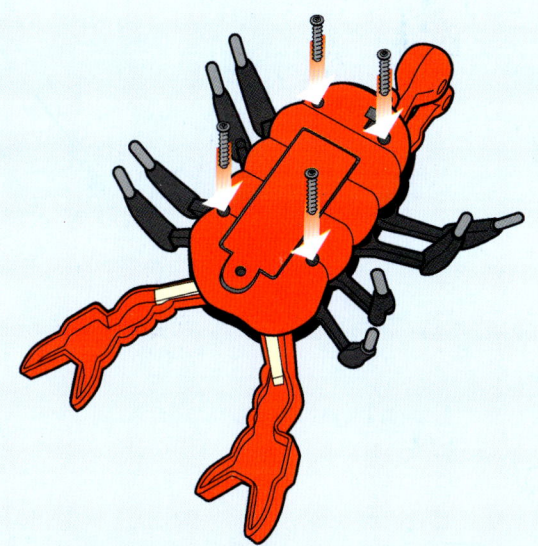

▸ Turn the scorpion over. Don't let go.

▸ Find the four screws you removed in step 1. Screw them back in to secure the top shell to the bottom shell.

29

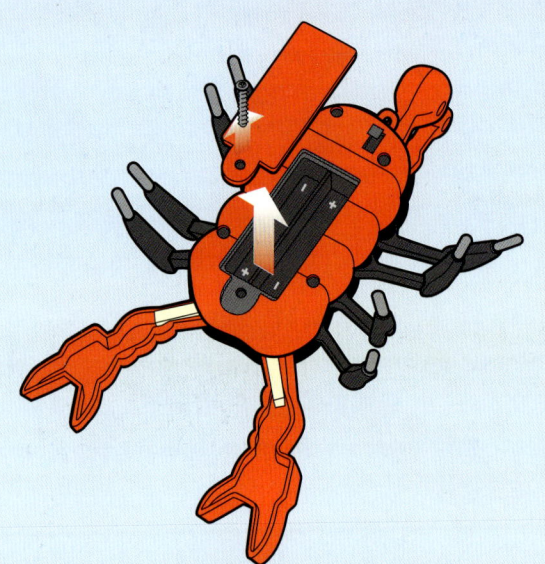
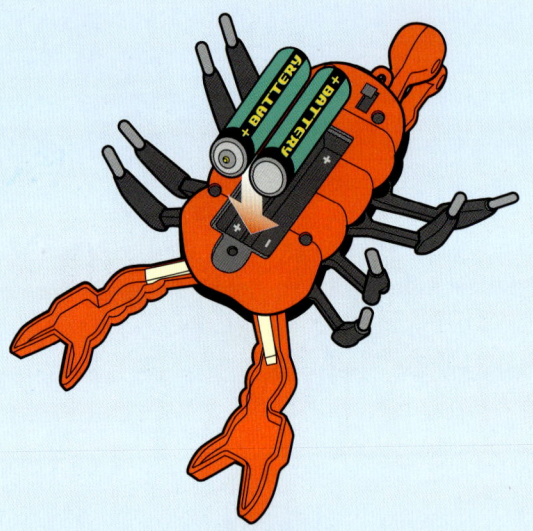

7. Insert the batteries

▸ Unscrew the battery compartment door and remove it.

▸ Insert two AAA batteries in the battery compartment according to the markings inside the compartment. Make sure you insert them the right way.

TIP: *You can attach the traction pads to the feet now or wait until you start experimenting (see page 32).*

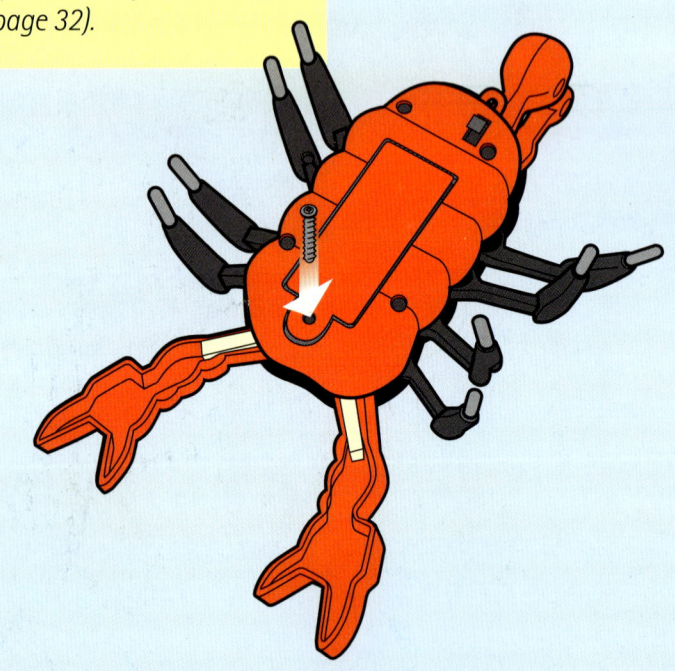

▸ Screw the battery compartment door back on.

Battery cautions

- To ensure proper safety and operation, the battery replacement must always be done by an adult.
- Never let a child use this product unless the battery door is secure.
- Keep all batteries away from small children, and immediately dispose of any batteries safely.
- Batteries are small objects and could be ingested.
- Nonrechargeable batteries are not to be recharged.
- Rechargeable batteries are to be removed from the toy before being charged.
- Rechargeable batteries are only to be charged under adult supervision.
- Different types of batteries or new and used batteries are not to be mixed.
- Only batteries of the same or equivalent types as recommended are to be used.
- Do not mix alkaline, standard (carbon-zinc), or rechargeable (nickel-cadmium) batteries.
- Batteries are to be inserted with the correct polarity.
- Exhausted batteries are to be removed from the toy.
- The supply terminals are not to be short-circuited.

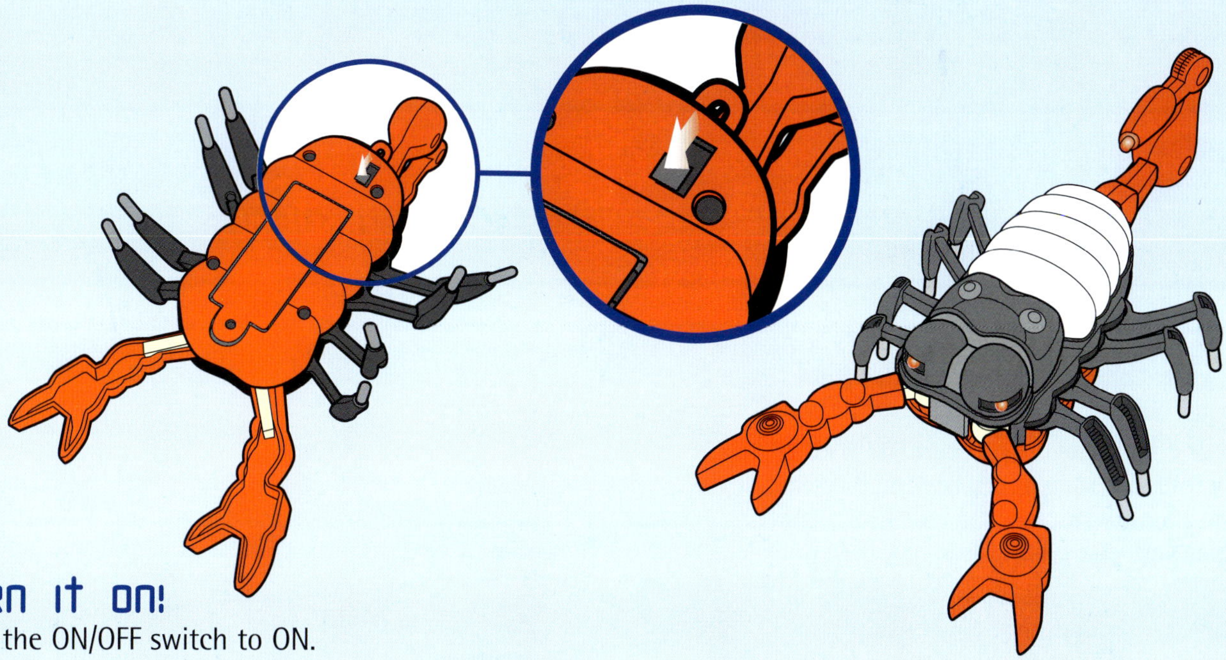

8. turn it on!

▸ Slide the ON/OFF switch to ON.
  (The switch is on the underside of the scorpion.)
▸ Stand the scorpion on its legs and watch it go!

troubleshooting

If you've followed these assembly instructions and your scorpion doesn't work right when you switch it on, follow these tips:

If your scorpion doesn't walk smoothly:

▸ Make sure no wires are caught in the leg mechanisms.
▸ Make sure the top and bottom shells are attached to each other securely.

If your scorpion's claws don't move:

▸ Make sure no wires are pressing against the claw/arm mechanism.

If your scorpion doesn't walk at all or the lights don't come on:

▸ Make sure the batteries are inserted correctly.
▸ Make sure the batteries are fresh.

taking it apart

▸ To take your scorpion apart, pull gently at the joints. In other words, to separate a claw from an arm, hold the parts as close to the joint as possible. Don't hold the scorpion's claw by the tip, for instance. Otherwise, parts could break.
▸ To remove legs, pry the pins out one at a time, then lift the legs off.

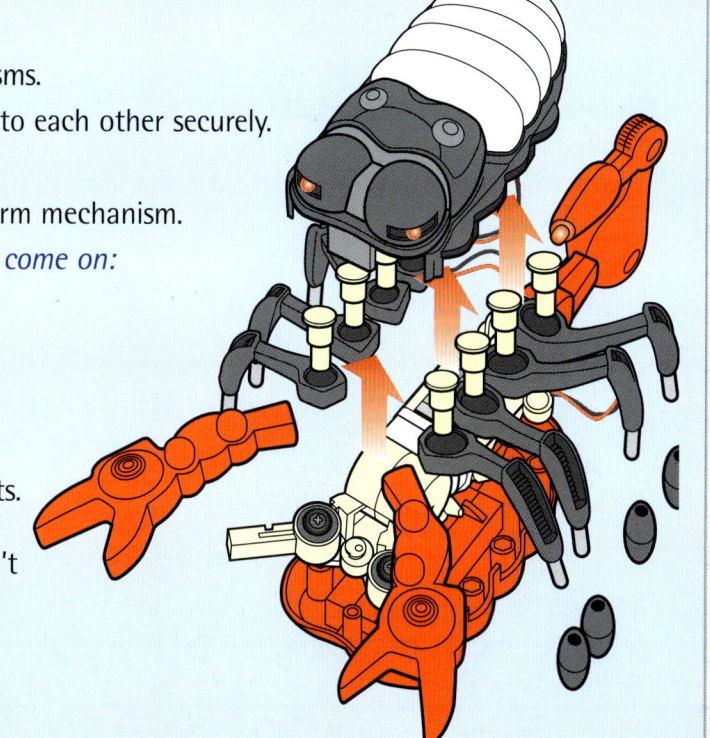

Robotic Scorpion Experiments

Your robotic scorpion is assembled. Your robot and scorpion knowledge is increased. Now it's time to try these activities and experiments to put your bot to the test.

Full Tilt
Can your robotic scorpion walk up an incline? Set it on a baking sheet or tray and find out. How steep can the surface be before the scorpion loses traction and slips? Change the surface and see if that affects how the scorpion walks on an incline. Can it walk on wax paper? Can it walk on sandpaper? How about newspaper? Turn the scorpion around so it's walking downhill. Can the scorpion keep its footing?

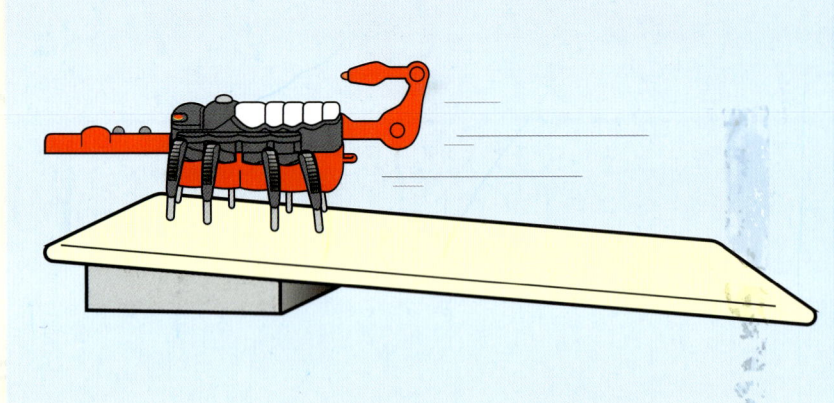

Drag Racing
Take advantage of your scorpion's hitch to see how much weight it can pull. Tie one end of a length of string, twine, or yarn to the hitch. Tie or clip small objects to the other end. Can your scorpion pull a pencil? Paper clips? A chain of paper clips? (How long a chain?) How many different objects can your scorpion drag at one time?

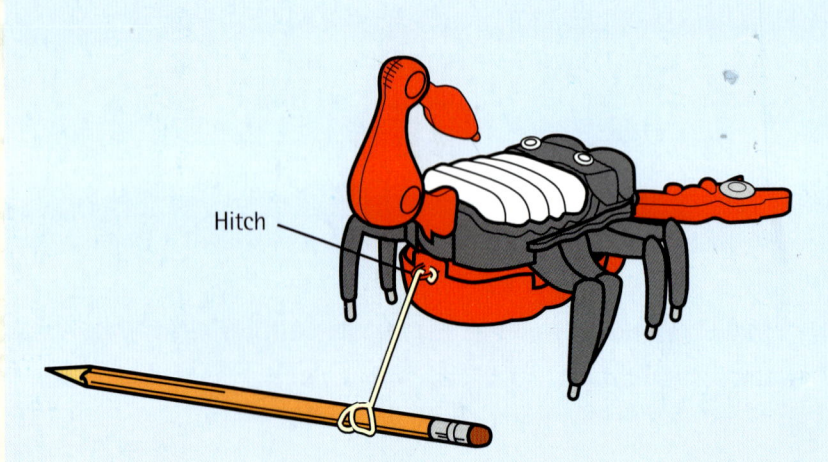

Best Foot Forward
Attach the traction pads to your scorpion's feet by inserting the feet into the hole in the pads. Does the scorpion walk faster with the pads or without them? Does it perform better on the other tests—walking on inclines, dragging weight—with the pads?

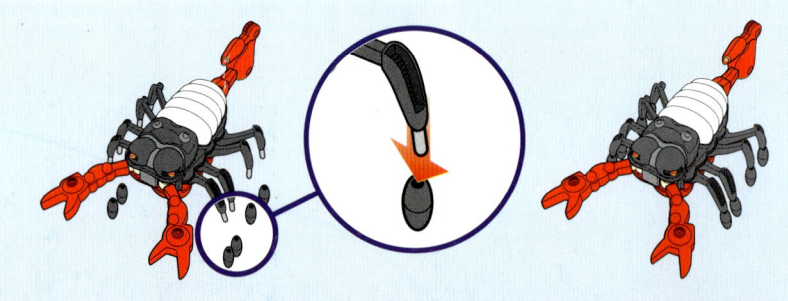